Sing a Song of Sixpence

Copyright © QED Publishing 2005

First published in the UK in 2005 by
QED Publishing
A Quarto Group Company
226 City Road
London EC1V 2TT
www.qed-publishing.co.uk

Reprinted in this format 2006

A Catalogue record for this book is
available from the British Library.

ISBN 1 84538 563 2

Compiled by Anne Faundez
Designed by Louise Morley
Illustrated by Simone Abel

Publisher Steve Evans
Creative Director Zeta Davies
Senior Editor Hannah Ray

Printed and bound in China

Sing a Song of Sixpence

Compiled by Anne Faundez

QED Publishing

Sing a Song of Sixpence

Sing a song of sixpence,
A pocket full of rye;
Four and twenty blackbirds
Baked in a pie.

When the pie was opened,
The birds began to sing;
Wasn't that a dainty dish
To set before the king?

The king was in his counting house,
Counting out his money;
The queen was in the parlour,
Eating bread and honey.

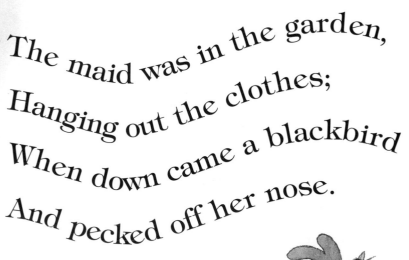

The maid was in the garden,
Hanging out the clothes;
When down came a blackbird
And pecked off her nose.

Little Jack Horner

Little Jack Horner sat in a corner

Eating his Christmas pie,

He put in his thumb and pulled out a plum,

And said...

"What a good boy am I!"

Little Miss Muffet

Little Miss Muffet
Sat on a tuffet,
Eating her curds and whey.

Along came a spider
Who sat down beside her,
And frightened Miss Muffet away.

Here We Go 'Round the Mulberry Bush

Here we go 'round the mulberry bush,
The mulberry bush, the mulberry bush,
Here we go 'round the mulberry bush,
On a cold and frosty morning.

This is the way we wash our hands,
Wash our hands, wash our hands,
This is the way we wash our hands,
On a cold and frosty morning.

This is the way we brush our teeth,
Brush our teeth, brush our teeth,
This is the way we brush our teeth,
On a cold and frosty morning.

This is the way we go to school,
Go to school, go to school,
This is the way we go to school,
On a cold and frosty morning.

One, Two, Three, Four, Five

One, two, three, four, five,
Once I caught a fish alive.
Six, seven, eight, nine, ten,
Then I let it go again.

Why did you let it go?
Because it bit my finger so.
Which finger did it bite?
This little finger on the right.

Two Little Dicky Birds

Two little dicky birds
Sitting on a wall;
One named Peter,
One named Paul.

Fly away, Peter!
Fly away, Paul!
Come back, Peter!
Come back, Paul!

Old King Cole

Old King Cole
Was a merry old soul,
And a merry old soul was he.
He called for his pipe,
And he called for his bowl,
And he called for his fiddlers three.

Cock a Doodle Doo!

Cock a doodle doo!
My dame has lost her shoe,
My master's lost his fiddling stick,
And doesn't know what to do.

Hush, Little Baby

Hush, little baby, don't say a word,
Mama's going to buy you a mocking-bird.

And if that mocking-bird don't sing,
Mama's going to buy you a diamond ring.

And if that diamond ring turns brass,
Mama's going to buy you a looking glass.

And if that looking glass gets broke,
Mama's going to buy you a billy goat.

And if that billy goat won't pull,
Mama's going to buy you a cart and bull.

And if that cart and bull turn over,
Mama's going to buy you a dog named Rover.

And if that dog named Rover won't bark,
Mama's going to buy you a horse and cart.

And if that horse and cart fall down,
You'll still be the sweetest little baby in town.

Girls and Boys Come Out to Play

Girls and boys come out to play,

The moon doth shine as bright as day,

Leave your supper and leave your sleep,

And join your playfellows in the street;

Come with a hoop, come with a call,

Come and be merry, or not at all,

Up the ladder and over the wall,

A penny loaf will serve us all.

Wee Willie Winkie

Wee Willie Winkie
Runs through the town,

Upstairs
and
downstairs

In his nightgown.
Rapping at the window,
Crying through the lock,
"Are the children all in bed,
For it's past eight o'clock?"

Hush-a-bye, Baby

Hush-a-bye, baby, on the tree top,

When the wind blows, the cradle will rock;

When the bough breaks, the cradle will fall,

Down will come baby, cradle, and all.

Sleep, Baby, Sleep

Sleep, baby, sleep;
Thy father guards the sheep,
Thy mother shakes the dreamland tree,
And from it fall sweet dreams for thee;
Sleep, baby, sleep.

Can you remember?

How many blackbirds were baked in a pie?

Can you remember the names of the two little dicky birds?

How many things did
Old King Cole call for?

Can you think of any words
that rhyme with "five"?

Can you name four things that Mama
will give her little baby?

Can you remember
who lost her shoe?

Can you describe a dream that you would like the dreamland tree to give you?

Who frightened Miss Muffet away?